Can you find the cheese among this crowd of skunks?

# Find the FARTER

WORDS BY
PHYLLIS F. HART
PICTURES BY
MIKE LAUGHEAD

sourcebooks
wonderland

I'm hiding in this library,
letting loose a fart.
But squeezing out a silent one
takes a special art.
Can you find me here somewhere?
Take a good, long look.
I might be hiding near a shelf,
or tooting near a book.

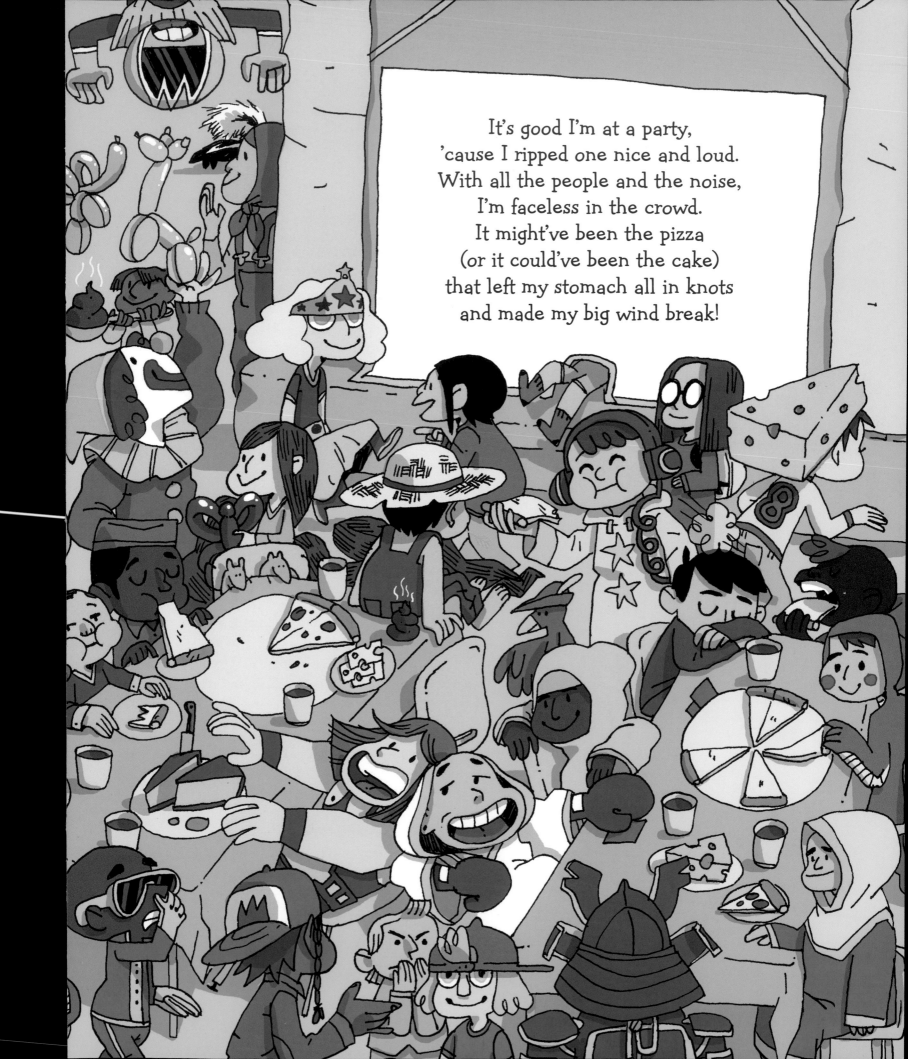

It's good I'm at a party,
'cause I ripped one nice and loud.
With all the people and the noise,
I'm faceless in the crowd.
It might've been the pizza
(or it could've been the cake)
that left my stomach all in knots
and made my big wind break!

It's quiet
in the gallery,
so I can't make
a sound...
Good thing my
fart's a silent one...
Look close,
can I be found?

I truly thought it would be fun
to fly up in a plane,
the sky so big, the earth so small—
much better than a train!
But now there's hardly room to breathe
all crammed in this small chair.
And now I've let a fart ring out into recycled air!

My mom tells me I need to eat
more vegetables and fruit.
I had some brussels sprouts for lunch,
and now I have to toot.
See, fruits and veggies give me gas—
and all my friends can tell.
They laugh with me about the sound,
until they get the smell...

Even with the heat today,
it's busy at the zoo.
These animals and humans stink—
it almost smells like poo!
The monkeys reek, the sloths do too—
you'd better hold your nose.
Hopefully, no one will know
when my butt tuba blows!

It's really crowded
up in here,
so I'll have to
keep it brief.
I farted once
(or maybe twice),
and it stinks
beyond belief!

Basketball's my favorite sport.
I love when players dunk!
But I'm about to toot my horn
and make it smell like skunk...
It's not the final whistle blow
or wildly roaring fans.
It's my proud, stinky, booty burp
that rattles all the stands!

I love the smell of baking bread and hearty lobster stew.
But farting in this fancy place is frowned upon—who knew?
It's not the onions or the fish that brings tears to my eye:
"Egad! Zat smell is 'orrible!" I hear the new chef cry.

I always give my bestest smile
on picture day at school.
"Say cheese!" the cameraman yells out,
and looks down at his stool.
Right as the camera flashes once,
I squeeze my cheeks real tight.
And "pffft!" out comes a hearty fart
that brings the group delight!

Nothing beats the smell of popcorn:
salty, fresh, and hot.
I only wish my farts could smell
that good, but they do not!
Instead, they smell like stinky fish
and sound like slurping pop.
Too bad for everyone around—
I just can't seem to stop!

I always thought a big greenhouse
would smell so fresh and clean,
but now I've made it smell so foul...
Can I leave unseen?

I'm scootin' and I'm tootin'
around this grocery store!
This gassy game makes shopping fun
instead of just a chore.
Oh sure, we pick up groceries,
like lettuce and some cheese,
but seeing someone smell my fart
makes shopping here a breeze.

I came out to the beach today
to swim and play in sand,
but didn't know the bubbles
that I made would be on land.
While playing catch and having fun,
I felt a bubble build.
I bopped back to my group of friends
before my pants were filled!

While aboard this grand spacecraft,
the *Gas Star 3-2-1*,
I felt a teeny tushy toot
squish out between my buns.
I tried to hold my fart inside,
but I could hardly stand it.
It blew as big as Uranus—
of course I mean the planet!

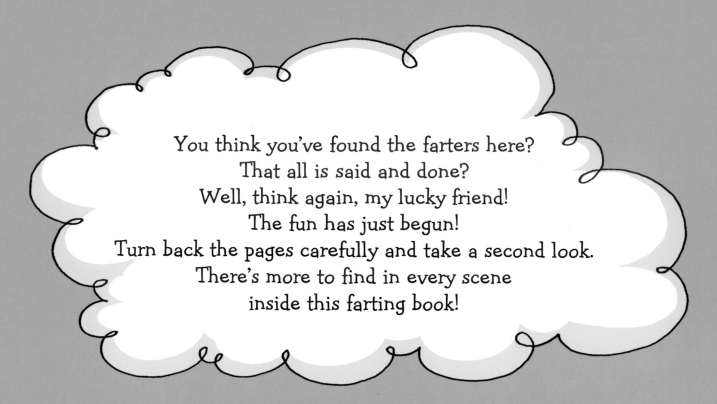

You think you've found the farters here?
That all is said and done?
Well, think again, my lucky friend!
The fun has just begun!
Turn back the pages carefully and take a second look.
There's more to find in every scene
inside this farting book!

Can you find these
on every page?

# A SKUNK

# A CAT

# TWO MICE

# SOMEONE CUTTING THE CHEESE

# A POOP PILE

Can you find the cheese among this crowd of skunks?